W9-BGL-979

Old Mother Hubbard's Stolen Bone

Crabtree Publishing Company

www.crabtreebooks.com

1-800-387-7650

PMB 59051, 350 Fifth Ave.
59ᵗʰ Floor,
New York, NY 10118

616 Welland Ave.
St. Catharines, ON
L2M 5V6

Published by Crabtree Publishing in 2013

Series editor: Louise John
Editors: Katie Powell, Kathy Middleton
Notes to adults: Reagan Miller
Cover design: Paul Cherrill
Design: D.R.ink
Consultant: Shirley Bickler
Production coordinator and
   Prepress technician: Margaret Amy Salter
Print coordinator: Katherine Berti

Text © Alan Durant 2009
Illustration © Leah-Ellen Heming 2009

First published in 2009 by Wayland
(A division of Hachette Children's Books)

Printed in the
U.S.A./092014/CG20140808

Library and Archives Canada
Cataloguing in Publication

CIP available at Library and Archives Canada

Library of Congress
Cataloging-in-Publication Data

CIP available at Library of Congress

Old Mother Hubbard's Stolen Bone

Written by Alan Durant

Illustrated by Leah-Ellen Heming

Crabtree Publishing Company

www.crabtreebooks.com

Old Mother Hubbard had a dog—
a very clever dog. He did tricks.
He could lie down with his paws
in the air and play dead.

He could dance and stand on his front paws. He could open doors and shut them again.

"What a clever boy!" said Old Mother Hubbard. How she loved that dog!

One day she went to the butcher's shop and bought her dog a big juicy bone for a treat. She put the bone in the cupboard.

Then she went out in the garden to hang the washing on the line.

When she came back, her dog
was doing cartwheels. Old Mother
Hubbard laughed.

"What a clever boy!" she said, and she
went to the cupboard to fetch her dog
the bone.

But when she opened the door, the cupboard was bare!
"I've been robbed!" she cried. Her poor dog covered his eyes with his paws and howled.

"Don't you worry, boy," said Old Mother Hubbard. "I'll catch that bone thief!"

Old Mother Hubbard ran out into the street and—oof! She bumped into Simple Simon. He was carrying something in a leather bag.

"Did you steal my bone?" Old Mother Hubbard demanded.

"Indeed, no!" said Simple Simon.
"I've got lots of bones of my own. See?"
He pointed to his head, his arms, and
his legs.

"Not those sort of bones," said Old
Mother Hubbard, annoyed.
"I mean the bone I bought for my dog
to eat." She glared at Simple Simon.
"Show me what's in your bag."

Simple Simon opened his bag and took out a chicken pie. "I bought it from a pieman going to the fair," he said. "It cost me one penny."

"Bah!" huffed Old Mother Hubbard, and on she ran.

At the corner of the street Little Jack Horner was sitting on the pavement eating.

When he saw Old Mother Hubbard, he hid the food behind his back.

"Did you steal my dog's bone?" cried Old Mother Hubbard.

"N-n-no," said Little Jack, frightened. "Not I."

"Show me what's behind your back,"
she commanded.

Little Jack Horner put his hands behind him
and brought out a Christmas pie.

Then he put in his thumb and pulled out a plum, and said, "What a good boy am I!"

"Bah!" huffed Old Mother Hubbard,
and on she ran.

Old Mother Hubbard came to Jack Sprat's house. He and his wife were sitting at the table munching.

Old Mother Hubbard put her head through the window.

"Are you eating my dog's bone?"
she demanded.
"Certainly not!" humphed Jack Sprat.
"I'm eating the lean of the meat."

"And I'm eating the fat," said his wife.
"But neither of us would ever eat bones!"
"Bah!" huffed Old Mother Hubbard.

Suddenly there was a commotion
behind her.

"Stop, thief!" someone shouted.

Old Mother Hubbard turned to see
the Knave of Hearts sprinting past her
carrying a basket. The queen was chasing
after him.

"Stop, thief!" the queen shouted again.

"I bet that naughty knave stole my dog's bone," said Old Mother Hubbard to herself. Off she ran after the knave and the queen.

Old Mother Hubbard and the queen chased the knave through the town, upstairs and downstairs, and into the lady's chamber...

over Margery Daw's seesaw...

and past lavender blue and lavender green...

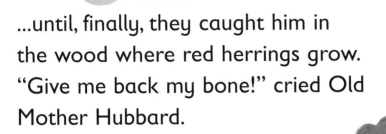

...until, finally, they caught him in the wood where red herrings grow. "Give me back my bone!" cried Old Mother Hubbard.

"But I didn't steal your bone," said the Knave of Hearts.

"No, you stole my tarts," said
the queen.

"Sorry," said the knave. "They were so
delicious, and I was very hungry."

The queen forgave the knave. "Since we're in the forest, we may as well have a picnic," she said, and she passed around the tarts.

"A very good idea," agreed Old Mother Hubbard.

So, Old Mother Hubbard, the queen, and the Knave of Hearts sat and ate until all the tarts were gone.

"It's still a mystery who stole that bone," said Old Mother Hubbard. But she was so full of delicious jam tarts that she wasn't really that bothered any more.

She said farewell and walked back home...

...and there was her dog, chewing his way through that stolen bone. What a naughty dog!

Notes for adults

Tadpoles: Nursery Crimes are structured for transitional and early fluent readers. The books may also be used for read-alouds or shared reading with younger children.

Tadpoles: Nursery Crimes are intended for children who are familiar with nursery rhyme characters and themes, but can also be enjoyed by anyone. Each story can be compared with the traditional rhyme, or appreciated for its own unique twist.

IF YOU ARE READING THIS BOOK WITH A CHILD, HERE ARE A FEW SUGGESTIONS:

1. Make reading fun! Choose a time to read when you and the child are relaxed and have time to share the story.

2. Before reading, invite the child to preview the book. The child can read the title, look at the illustrations, skim through the text, and make predictions as to what will happen in the story. This activity stimulates curiosity and promotes critical thinking skills.

3. During reading, encourage the child to monitor his or her understanding by asking questions to draw conclusions, making connections, and using context clues to understand unfamiliar words.

4. After reading, ask the child to review his or her predictions. Were they correct? Discuss different parts of the story, including main characters, setting, main events, the problem and solution. Challenge the child to retell the story in his or her own words to enhance comprehension.

5. Give praise! Children learn best in a positive environment.

VISIT THE LIBRARY AND CHECK OUT THESE RELATED NURSERY RHYMES AND CHILDREN'S SONGS:

Old Mother Hubbard
Simple Simon
Little Jack Horner

Jack Sprat
The Queen of Hearts
See-Saw, Margery Daw

Lavender's Blue
The Man in the Wilderness

IF YOU ENJOYED THIS BOOK, WHY NOT TRY ANOTHER TADPOLES: NURSERY CRIMES STORY?

Humpty Dumpty's Great Fall   *978-0-7787-8028-1 RLB*   *978-0-7787-8039-7 PB*
Little Bo Peep's Missing Sheep   *978-0-7787-8029-8 RLB*   *978-0-7787-8040-3 PB*
Little Miss Muffet's Big Scare   *978-0-7787-8030-4 RLB*   *978-0-7787-8041-0 PB*

VISIT WWW.CRABTREEBOOKS.COM FOR OTHER CRABTREE BOOKS.